GAMERS' GUIDE

By Luke Peterschmidt

SCHOLASTIC INC.

NEW YORK   TORONTO   LONDON   AUCKLAND
SYDNEY   MEXICO CITY   NEW DELHI   HONG KONG

ISBN 978-0-545-17761-0

12 11 10 9 8 7 6 5 4 3 2 1   10 11 12 13 14 15/0

Printed in the U.S.A.   40
First printing, May 2010

Hello, Bakugan fans! Welcome to this strategy guide. This book is designed to help make you a Bakugan master.

We all love to collect Bakugan, talk about Bakugan, and draw Bakugan all over our notebooks. But if you want to be a Bakugan master, that won't be enough! You'll need to know all the rules, be able to identify Bakugan, and develop strategies for using your Bakugan and cards. This guide is here to help! All the info inside comes straight from an expert Bakugan brawler. With these tips and a little practice, you'll be on your way.

So, have fun! And get ready to brawl!

CONTENTS

WHAT YOU NEED TO KNOW

This section covers the topics that every Bakugan master-in-training should know inside and out. From the basic rules, to more complicated multiplayer and "Big Game" versions, and more. Once you've memorized this section, you'll be well on your way!

BASIC RULES

The Basics

Before you can become a Bakugan master, you must learn how to brawl. This section reviews everything you need to know how to play correctly. If you need more help with the basics, head over to www.bakugan.com. The website has tons of helpful videos and other resources to help you learn the game correctly.

What You Need to Play

3 Gate cards (1 each of gold, silver, and copper), 3 Ability cards (1 each of red, green, and blue), and any 3 Bakugan. You may also use a mix of up to two Traps and/or Battle Gear (new in season 3).

Set-up

Sit across from your opponent and set up your game as shown below. Your cards, and Bakugan, (and Traps/Gear if you are playing with them)

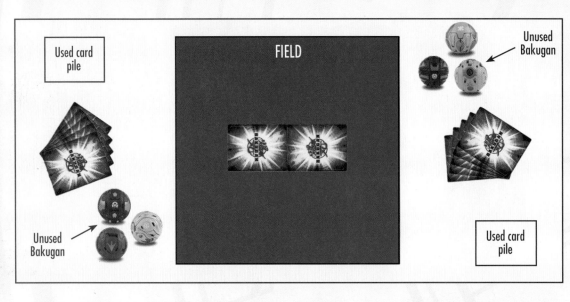

go to your right in your "unused pile." Your cards should be facedown so your opponent can't see them, but you may look at them any time you wish. Your "used pile" is to your left, and it's where game pieces go after they are…used. The field is where the battling takes place!

"Gate Card Set!"

On any turn that starts with no Gate cards in field (like the first one), each player takes one of their unused Gate cards and places it in front of their opponent so that they barely touch each other.

"Bakugan Brawl!"

The youngest player goes first and takes a Bakugan from their unused pile and rolls it toward the Gate cards in the field. Several things can happen . . . If the Bakugan doesn't open on a Gate card, it's a miss.

The Bakugan is put into its owner's used pile and it's now the other player's turn to roll. If it "stands" (opens) on a Gate card that doesn't already have a Bakugan on it, then it stays there and it's now the other player's turn. If it stands on a Gate card where that player already has one of his own Bakugan standing, then he must move that Bakugan to another Gate card where he doesn't already have a Bakugan.

If that move puts the Bakugan on a Gate card with an enemy's standing Bakugan, then there is a BATTLE!

If the player can't move their Bakugan (only 1 Gate card out, or the other Gate card already has one of their Bakugan standing on it), then he wins that Gate card and puts the card and both Bakugan into his used pile.

It's now the other player's turn. If it stands on a Gate card with an enemy's Bakugan, there is a BATTLE!

BATTLE!

Battle between two Bakugan follows these simple steps:

- Remove the Bakugan from the Gate card and read their G-Powers
- Flip the Gate card over and do whatever the text tells you to do
- Players can play any unused Ability cards that start with "Play during a battle" and do whatever they say. After playing, the Ability card is put in the owner's used pile.
- After both players are done playing Ability cards, each player's Bakugan gets a "Gate Attribute Bonus." Simply match the color of a Bakugan to the color symbols on the Gate card and add that number to the Bakugan's G-Power.
- The battle is won by the Bakugan who has the highest G-Power after Gate Attribute Bonuses are added.
- If there is a tie, the battle is won by the first Bakugan that stood on the Gate card.

The winning player takes his Bakugan and the Gate card and puts them both in his used pile. The losing player takes his Bakugan and puts it in his used pile. Then it is the other player's turn to roll.

The first player to get three Gate cards into their used pile wins!

Bakugan Traps

You may play an unused Trap in any battle where you have a Bakugan whose Attributes match the Attribute of the Trap you are playing. Drop the Trap on the Gate card to open it. You may then change the Attribute of your Bakugan to any Attribute revealed on the inside of the Trap.

Traps and Gear move like Bakugan. After a battle, they go to their owner's used pile. When you have no more Bakugan to roll, all of your used Bakugan and Traps move to your unused pile.

Ability Cards

Ability cards can be played at all sorts of different times in the game depending on which card it is. To see when an Ability card can be played, read the first sentence in the text box. To see what effect an Ability card will have in the game, read the rest of the text box.

GUIDE TO GOOD SPORTSMANSHIP

I spent almost a year touring around America and Canada teaching kids how to play Bakugan correctly as part of the Ultimate Bakugan Battle Tour. I met tens of thousands of Bakugan players and their parents. One thing I stressed at every stop was the importance of good sportsmanship. Not only because it's the right thing to do, but also because if you want to be a Bakugan master, you'll need to play a lot of different people, and who wants to play against a bad sport? If you lose, don't forget: Every loss is a chance to improve your strategy for the next game!

And one more thing: Remember that at the end of the game, all Bakugan go back to their owner! Taking another kid's Bakugan for keeps is definitely not good sportsmanship!

Gear, Power Level, and Special Evolution

Season 3 brought in three new concepts; Powerful Battle Gear that deploy directly onto your Bakugan, an ever increasing Power Level which allows you to play more and more powerful Ability cards, and the super high G-Power Special Evolution Bakugan. For more information on these, check out the season 3 rulebook over at www.bakugan.com.

Traps may look complicated, but using them in play is really simple!

You may include up to one Trap along with your three Bakugan. If you are playing the "Big Game," you may include up to two Traps along with your six Bakugan.

Your Traps start in the unused pile with your Bakugan. You may play a Trap in any battle as long as you have a Bakugan in the battle and the Trap is the same Attribute as your Bakugan in play.

When you play the Trap onto the Gate card, it will pop open and reveal one or more Attribute icons. You can switch the Attribute of your Bakugan to any of those new revealed icons!

After the battle, put any Traps you used into the used pile.

Whenever you run out of Bakugan to roll and need to move them from the used pile to the unused pile, you may move any Traps in the used pile to the unused pile as well.

TRAP SPECIAL CARDS

In addition to the basic Trap ability described above, each Trap comes with a special Ability card. You don't have to use these cards as one of your Ability card choices, but you may want to consider it. These cards can give you an edge:

Normally, Traps are best when played on an enemy Gate card, where you are not likely to be getting a very good Gate bonus. But sometimes you need a little more G-Power to win a battle on a Gate card where you already have a big bonus.

This is where a card like Fire Scorpion can make all the difference.

Sometimes you're in a close battle where you'd rather that no one got a Gate bonus. If that happens to you, try using Falcon Fly!

And sometimes, you are so far behind, you don't even want the battle to count! If that's the case, look to Legionoid.

ADVANCED RULES

Multiplayer Rules

You have probably noticed that the basic rules only cover a two-player game. If more than two of you want to play, use the following rules.

How Gate Cards Are Played

When three or more players play the game, each player plays their card as far away from themselves as they can in the middle of the field, touching the other players' cards. Here is the layout for a four-player game:

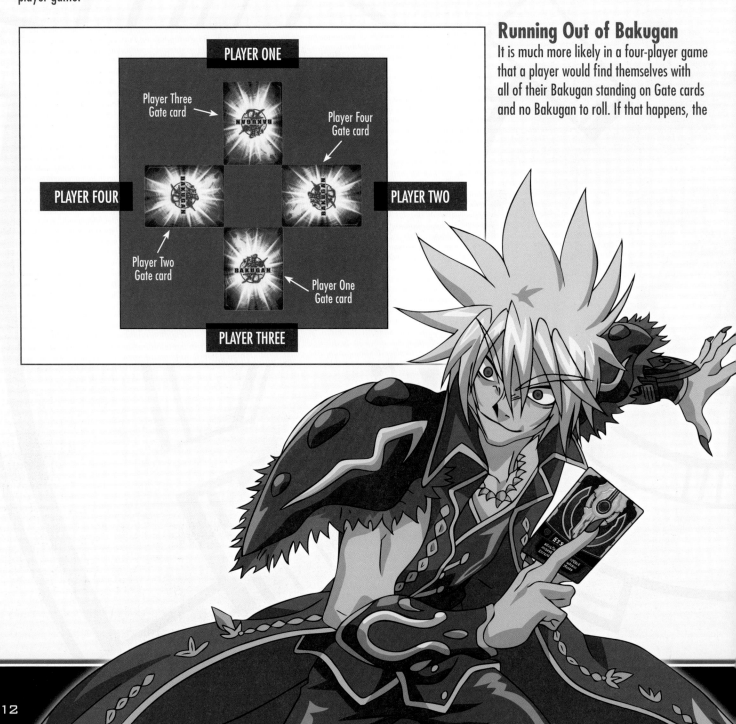

PLAYER ONE

Player Three Gate card

Player Four Gate card

PLAYER FOUR

PLAYER TWO

Player Two Gate card

Player One Gate card

PLAYER THREE

Turn Sequence

Randomly determine who goes first, second, third, fourth, etc. Players then sit in that order around the field just like in the diagram below.

Playing Cards

Players in a multiplayer game can only play Ability cards that get played before, after, or during a battle when they actually have a Bakugan in battle! Cards that can be played outside of battle can be played by any player. If two players want to play a card at the same time, the player whose turn is next gets the first chance to play their card.

Running Out of Bakugan

It is much more likely in a four-player game that a player would find themselves with all of their Bakugan standing on Gate cards and no Bakugan to roll. If that happens, the player may take one of their Bakugan off a Gate card and roll it. If the Bakugan lands on a card with another of his Bakugan on it, the player wins that Gate card without a battle.

Winning the Game

Winning the game is exactly the same as the two-player version. The first player to get three Gate cards to their used pile wins!

Odd Situations

Some very unusual and strange things can pop up in a multiplayer game. If a situation arises that is not covered in these rules, the players at the table should take a quick vote or flip a coin so that the game can keep moving forward. After the game, players can go to the www.bakugan.com and ask the question in the forums. That way, you'll be prepared the next time you play!

THE BIG GAME

The Big Game version of Bakugan doubles everything. Instead of using three Bakugan, you use six. Instead of using up to one Trap, you can use up to two. Instead of three Gate cards and three Ability cards, you get six of each (two of each color). Winning the game requires six Gate cards in your used pile. And yes, it's double the fun.

The game is set up like this:

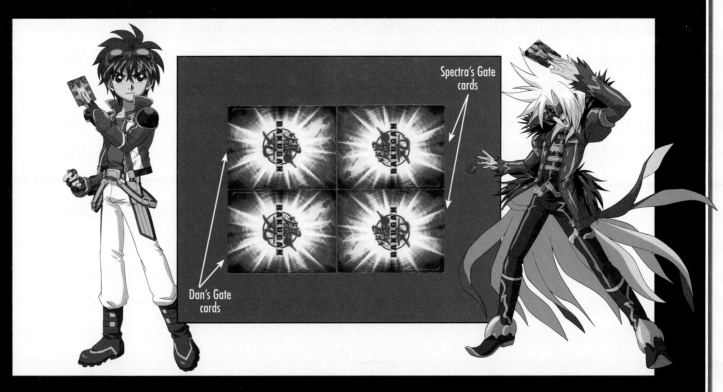

Spectra's Gate cards

Dan's Gate cards

All the other rules of the game are the same. You don't put out new Gate cards until all the ones in the field have been won, and when you do, you put out two more.

If you're really adventurous, you could even try the Big Game multiplayer-style!

STRATEGY SECTION

Attribute strategy is key to improving your Bakugan game. This section can help you strategize with your favorite Bakugan Attribute, as well as all of the other Attributes, so you'll be ready for anything. You'll even learn about playing more than one Attribute in the same game. Just as important, by paying close attention to this section, you'll know what type of tricks your opponent is likely to use based on which Attribute he is playing.

PYRUS

Attributes are an incredibly important aspect of Bakugan strategy. The Attributes can be directly traced back to the universe of Vestroia, where all Bakugan reside. In Vestroia, there are six planets: Pyrus, Aquos, Haos, Darkus, Subterra, and Ventus. The unique environment of each planet creates different strengths and skills. Pyrus, for example, is a hot, volcanic planet. This means that Bakugan with a Pyrus Attribute are likely to be good with fire and flame-based attacks. They also tend to be very powerful—it has been said that they draw their intense strength and energy from the planet's deep molten gorges.

Pyrus strategy is all about knowing how to use the power of your fiery Bakugan. You want to get into battles at just the right time to leverage your fiery intensity to its greatest effect!

THE PYRUS BAKUGAN

There are many Pyrus Bakugan, and for game play, most are just as good as others. The exceptions are those Bakugan that get a special bonus from their very own, specific card:

If you've got a card that mentions a specific Bakugan, then be sure to include both in your force.

THE GATE CARDS

Silver

Look for a card that not only gives a great bonus for Pyrus, but that also doesn't give too high a bonus for anyone else. Any of these would be good choices:

"Every Bakugan master had to lose many games to get better."

Bakugan Tournament Master Ray

Gold

You could pick a card like Hades, as long as you make sure you include a Pyrus version of the card. Another option would be Forest Fire. It's a little tricky to use, but worth it. This card barely gives a bonus to Pyrus, so you'll probably lose the first fight, but once it goes into your opponent's used pile, it'll give your other Pyrus Bakugan a G-Power bonus for the rest of the game! This makes it a great Gate card to play first.

Copper

Two of my favorites are Field of Flames and Stand Off. If I plan to play my Ability cards early in the game, I'll use Stand Off and make it the last Gate card I play. If I plan to play my Ability cards later, I'll play Field of Flames, hoping that my opponent has already played a few — giving me that extra bonus.

Red

If you're an experienced and accurate roller, try Dan's Throw. It's a great choice if you want to play a particular Ability card twice. If you still haven't mastered your rolling skills, a re-rolling card would be a solid choice. Pyrus also features a lot of red Ability cards that help you get into battles when you want to, like Magnetic Action and Flames of Light.

Blue

The blue cards are mostly about big G-Power bonuses, so using the biggest one you have is often a good strategy. It's worth noting, though, that as the G-Power bonuses on these cards go up, they are harder to play. For example, the 140 G-Power you get from Brushfire can only be used on battles on your own Gate cards. Personally, I like the cards that give big bonuses on my opponent's Gate cards, because that's usually when I need the help!

Green

One of the best of the tricky green Ability cards is Pyrus. This card is best for fighting friends who have very large G-Power Bakugan, particularly on your own Gate cards. And don't overlook cards like Shadowfire and Dynamo Charge! Both can really turn a battle.

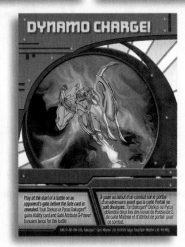

Sometimes, Ability card strategy can seem overwhelming. But remember: there are lots of clues on the cards that will help. And the best way to figure out what works for you is to keep trying new strategies. You might lose while working on a new maneuver, but every loss will give you clues to improve your strategy and become a better player.

THE MANY FACES OF DRAGO

There are many famous Pyrus Bakugan, but none more so than Dan's own Dragonoid. Drago appears in many different evolutions throughout seasons 1 and 2, and some brand-new ways in season 3. See how many different Dragonoids you can name!

DRAGONOID

ULTIMATE DRAGONOID

NEO DRAGONOID

POPULAR PYRUS BRAWLERS

DAN

Dan is the most famous Pyrus brawler, and the leader of the Bakugan Brawlers Resistance. At the start of season 2, he returns to save New Vestroia from the Vestals. His Bakugan is Drago, and in season 2 he also uses a Scorpion Trap that was given to him by Mira.

CHAN

At one point Chan was the third-ranked brawler. Her guardian Bakugan was Pyrus Fortress. Dan beat Chan in a duel early in season 1, but she remained active and saved Joe from Hal-G.

SPECTRA

He is Vexos' most powerful brawler. His guardian Bakugan is a Pyrus Viper Helios and he matches it with a Metalfencer Trap. In season 2 he is unmasked and revealed to be Keith, Mira's older brother.

DARKUS

The Darkus planet is located in a dark hemisphere of the Vestroia universe. Darkus Bakugan are used to fighting in the shadows, and thrive in battles where their opponents can't see what's coming at them!

Darkus is all about surprising your opponents by taking away their options. Your Ability cards in particular can be stunningly frustrating for your opponents, crippling their best-laid plans.

THE DARKUS BAKUGAN

Unless you have a specific trick in mind for a particular battle, you'll probably want to pick at least two high G-Power Bakugan. You might want to pick one lower G-Power Bakugan in case your opponent is playing any Gate cards that allow the lowest power Bakugan to win. You should have enough control over which Bakugan fight at which cards to use your low-G-Power Bakugan to great effect.

THE GATE CARDS

Silver

Usually for silver Gate cards, you should look for a card that not only gives a great bonus for your Attribute, but one that also doesn't give too high a bonus for any other Attribute. I also often pick a card with a high Darkus bonus and a low highlighted bonus, like Dusk or Haunted Night. This is because sometimes I'll use an Ability card like Darkus 2 to change my opponent's Attribute to the highlighted one — a classic Darkus move.

Gold

Gold Gate cards are where you usually look for cards that match one or more of your Bakugan and have a good Attribute bonus. I have one Darkus force that uses most of its Ability cards early in the game, so I include Holding Power for its big bonus. I sometimes use Lighting Field, particularly when I'm playing a multiplayer game and there is a good chance that I've got a Brontes standing somewhere else.

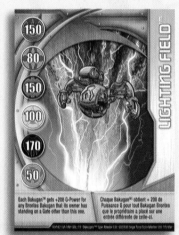

Copper

Copper cards often let you come from behind, but you'll need to be careful with popular cards like Duck & Win and Tricky Gate, as they have pretty big Darkus Attribute bonuses. I like to use Darkness Chamber or Spectrum Null Gate if I don't have all huge G-Power Bakugan, as the cards both fit in with the general theme of limiting what my opponent can do.

THE ABILITY CARDS

Red

You have lots of choices for great red Darkus cards. Dark Snap gives you a bonus each time your enemy plays an Ability card. If you're an experienced roller, Dark Snap can shut down all Gate and Ability bonuses. Masquerade's Launcher can be used to change your enemy's Attribute (good when they are on their own Gate card). And if all else fails, there's always Clean Slate—your Bakugan reset button!

"The path to become a Bakugan master is filled with experimentation."

Bakugan Tournament Master Cartson

Blue

For blue Ability cards, consider choosing those you can use on your opponent's Gate cards, like Power From Darkness. In multiplayer games, Shade is a good option, as it works on all Gate cards. There's also Triangle of Power, which combines seamlessly with Clean Slate.

Green

Make sure any green Ability card fits with your overall strategy. For instance, Darkness to Victory is a fantastic card if you are willing to lose your first battle: Making your opponent play his Gate cards face up can give you a huge edge. Shadow Vortex, on the other hand, is a great card to stop your opponent from getting a huge Gate bonus.

Darkus is fun to play, but like all Attributes, it takes practice and time to get a handle on the more advanced tactics of when to play your cards. But once you have it down, you'll find that when you win, you'll win handily. But, keep in mind that Darkus has some trouble against straightforward fighting Attributes like Subterra or Pyrus, as they do not rely too much on a single trick to win the game.

THE DOOM CARD!

The Doom card is the most famous card in the entire Bakugan universe. It is a powerful card, but also a dangerous one. The card gives a small Darkus G-Power bonus, but the real power behind the card is that it can send an enemy's Bakugan to the Doom Dimension, removing it from the game. Be careful, though! If you lose the battle, it's your Bakugan that will be gone from the game.

DOOM CARD

30

Play at the start of a battle. The losing player's Bakugan™ is removed from the game. Your Bakugan™ gains G-Power based on its Attribute.

Joue au début de la bataille. Le Bakugan™ du joueur perdant sera retiré de la partie. Ton Bakugan™ obtient les points de Puissance G de la carte selon son Attribut.

BA178-AB-SM Bakugan™ 2008 Spin Master LTD. & SEGA Toys 46/48

POPULAR DARKUS BRAWLERS

MASQUERADE
In season 1, Masquerade was the key Darkus brawler. He continually tried to send Bakugan to the Doom Dimension—he even sent his very first guardian Bakguan Darkus Reaper to the Doom Dimension. He got a new Guardian with Darkus Hyrdanoid. Late in season 1 it was revealed that Masquerade was really Alice!

ACE
Ace is a member of the Bakugan Brawlers Resistance in season 2. Though he and Dan have arguments, they always make up in the end. His guardian is a Darkus Percival and his main Trap is a Falcon Fly.

SHADOW
Shadow is the youngest member of Vexos, and has the unique ability to copy other people's voices, which he uses to lure members of the Bakugan Brawlers Resistance into Traps. His guardian Bakugan is a Darkus Hades, and he uses a Fortress as his main Trap.

AQUOS

Deep below the surface of the water planet's depths lurk deadly Aquos Bakugan. Masters of liquid environments, Aquos Bakugan move seamlessly from one attack to another. Surefooted on the most slippery ground and always on the move, they quickly evaluate their opponents' weaknesses—and then strike.

Aquos strategy is all about patience and creativity. You have to think ahead, and wait for just the right moment to play your strategy.

THE AQUOS BAKUGAN

You really can't go wrong with any choice of Aquos Bakugan. Always make sure to use one high G-Power Bakugan to handle the straight-forward fights, but the other two can be medium or even low G-power, depending on your card choices. More than other Attributes, your choice of Bakugan will be dependent on which cards you plan to use.

THE GATE CARDS

Since you might be able to reuse a Gate card, your choice of Gate cards is very important.

Silver

Aquos can get away with risky cards like Whirlpool, which give really good bonuses to Aquos, but also decent bonuses to other Attributes. It can be a bit of a gamble, but Aquos Bakugan are experts at avoiding fights if necessary. Deep Cave is also a worthwhile choice if you know what your opponent will be playing — or if you put in the ability to change your enemies' Attributes in battle.

Gold

If you can find it, Power Up is fantastic for Aquos. It came out in an early Battle Pack, but it is worth tracking down. I've had this card give me a 440 G-Power boost on several occasions! You can also choose a gold card that matches one or more of your Bakugan, which is particularly helpful if you have an Aquos Frosch — a card that can help you take an enemy's Ability card. Just make sure to play it when you have no unused green or blue Ability cards.

Copper

For Aquos, check out copper cards that only work in very specific situations, like Pounce, which punishes a player for having a Bakugan of the same Attribute in their used pile. It is a tough card to pull off, but powerful. Lock & Load is great if you plan to play all of your Ability cards early. Low Bridge is another solid choice as long as you're playing at least one low G-Power Bakugan.

Red

Marionette ensures your opponent's Bakugan lands on a Gate card where you'll be at a big advantage, like putting his high G-Power Bakugan on a Gate card where the lowest G-Power Bakugan wins. If using a Tripod Trap, which is a common Aquos choice, Prismatic Magnifier helps to get the most out of any Gate bonuses. With good Gate card selection, History Lesson can also be super powerful; just play it later in the game.

Blue

If I'm using Pounce, I try to include Triangle of Power: they make a powerful combo. While building an Ability card strategy around bonuses on your enemies' Gate cards is usually the way to go, Aquos often do better by winning on their own Gate cards, which is why I like Water Gun as well, particularly in multiplayer games.

Green

Aquos gets a lot of power from the green cards. Aquos 2 is a great way to fix a bad matchup. Flowing Waters is a great way to reuse a Gate card later in the game, particularly if you have a Gate card you want to use twice—or one you'd rather not use, like a risky silver card.

Playing against a great Aquos player is probably the best way to appreciate just how sneaky they can be. When playing Aquos yourself, you have to always be thinking a few rolls ahead to set up your big combos, but when they work, they are nearly unstoppable! It's also important to remember that you can be behind in Gate cards and still be very much in the game when playing Aquos, as your force should get better as more pieces are added to the used piles.

"Creating Bakugan clubs is a great way to continue your training!"

Bakugan Tournament Master Josh

AQUOS ON THE MOVE

A lot of players overlook cards that don't give G-Power bonuses—ones that "just" move things around. This can be a mistake, because these cards are deceptively powerful! Water Snap is a good example. The easiest battles to win are those on your own Gate cards, and Water Snap ensures that you get your Gate cards out faster than your opponent, and provides one of the best possible advantages to you—fighting on your Gate cards more often. Serious Aquos masters know how to put these cards to use.

WATER SNAP

Play before you roll an Aquos Bakugan® *if there is only one Gate card in the field.* Put one of your unused Gate cards in the field.

Joue avant de lancer un Bakugan® Aquos *s'il n'y a qu'une seule carte d'entrée sur le champ de bataille.* Place une de tes cartes d'entrée inutilisées sur le champ de bataille.

POPULAR AQUOS BRAWLERS

MARUCHO

Marucho is a key member of the Bakugan Brawlers Resistance. He uses his book smarts to create winning Aquos strategies. When he first arrived in New Vestroia, he had lost his guardian Bakugan Preyas, but he found a new one in Aquos Elfin. His Trap Bakugan is a Tripod Epsilon.

KLAUS

One of the Aquos battlers from season 1, Klaus was the one responsible for sending Marucho's Aquos Preyas into the Doom Dimension, but gave him back later. Klaus has been known to battle with an Aquos Sirenoid.

MYLENE

Mylene does things her own way. She became the leader of Vexos after Spectra and Gus traveled to Earth. Her guardian Bakugan is an Aquos Elico and her Trap is an Aquos Tripod Theta.

VENTUS

The planet of Ventus is swift and silent, but within its borders, violent storms rage.
Ventus Bakugan are like these storms—fast and deceptively strong.
Ventus Bakugan use their speed to confuse their enemies, and while their opponents
are off-balance, they strike with deadly force. As the fastest of all Bakugan,
they can never be counted out of a fight.

Ventus is all about moving power around. When your enemy braces for a strike from the left, a surprise hits them from the right. The key to winning with Ventus is to take advantage of situations that arise in most games. You'll be better off if you resist the urge to clobber your opponent head-on. Instead, be patient and wait for the perfect opportunity to make your move—and win.

THE VENTUS BAKUGAN

If you are going to play an all-Ventus force, you'll want to use at least one large G-Power Bakugan. I like to play with a large G-Power, a medium G-Power, and a low G-Power Bakugan, which provides maximum flexibility. So much of Ventus is about getting the best matchups you can, so having a wide selection of Bakugan available is usually best.

THE GATE CARDS

Silver

Picking a silver Gate card that gives a great bonus for Ventus, but one that also doesn't give too much to other Attributes, is critical for every Attribute, but even more so for Ventus. You'll want to track down a copy of The Spires or Ocean Spray if possible. Why is this so critical for Ventus? Keep reading . . .

Gold

For your gold Gate card, you can go a couple of different ways. I like to use Beneficial Wind, which can be dangerous, so I also use a Trap to change my Attribute to Subterra if needed. Skyress is also an excellent choice, as it lets you play all of your Ability cards, then get them all back at the end of the battle along with any your opponent played. And, of course, you can always use a gold Gate card that matches one or more of your Bakugan.

Copper

For your copper Gate card, you'll want to use a card that swaps printed G-Power — like G-Power Swap — or one where the lowest G-Power Bakugan wins, like Limbo Gate. With a range of Ventus Bakugan and the ability to move them around, you can really capitalize on these cards. Blurred Heat is also another great way to get to use Ability cards again.

The Ability cards for Ventus are a bit different than others as success is not necessarily linked to straight-up power bonuses. This means that using your cards the right way, at the right time, will take some skill. You'll need to keep track of what Bakugan are in used piles and which cards have been played so far. With practice, you should be able to do this easily. Just like rolling, it seems hard when you start, but gets easier with practice.

Red

Magnetic Action is a good choice for a red Ability card: it can drag an enemy Bakugan onto a Gate card that puts it at a disadvantage. This is great when your enemy rolls a really low G-Power Bakugan, as it's likely he's trying to get it on a card where the lower G-Power Bakugan has the edge. If your rolling is already solid, Gate Shift is one of the few red cards that can give a G-Power bonus when fighting on an enemy's Gate card.

"Trading is probably the best way to get the cards you need for a good force, so be sure to bring some extra cards with you!"

Bakugan Tournament Master Cartson

Blue

Generally useful G-Power boost blue cards are a fine selection, particularly Bronz Launcher — sometimes you get a double bonus! I also like Triangle of Power, as it gives big bonuses when played at the right time.

Green

For green Ability cards, try to use any cards that move things around: cards, Bakugan, Traps, etc., like Ventus and Ventus 2. These cards let a player swap the Gate card he's fighting over with one from his used pile or one from the opponent's used pile. This is a super tricky and powerful ability.

Ventus is fun to play. It's full of twists and turns that make each game surprising. You need to think ahead and plan moves, but when everything works as planned, it's very rewarding! Ventus does especially well against Subterra and Pyrus, but has some difficulties with Haos.

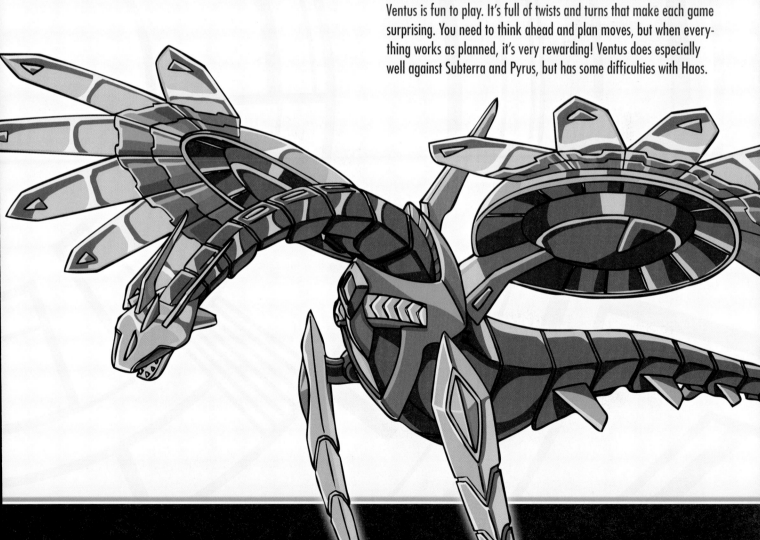

VENTUS BIG GAME AND MULTIPLAYER POWER

Because Ventus are so good at moving things around, they are particularly good in games where there are more Gate cards in the field. In the Big Game or a four-player game, there are twice as many Gate cards in play, and that's when Ventus strategy can become even more powerful! Try these cards next time:

Gale Force + a Trap like Dynamo to change your Attribute to Pyrus after you get the movement bonus.

Move everyone to places they don't want to be!

Get your Bakugan to your own Gate card—something very hard to do in a multiplayer game— or start a fight when your opponent lands on your gate!

POPULAR VENTUS BRAWLERS

SHUN

A former number-one-ranked player, Shun is now an important part of the Bakugan Brawlers Resistance. He lives with his grandfather, who used to be a famous ninja. He has used both Skyress and Ingram as guardian Bakugan. His preferred Trap is a Hylash.

LYNC

Lync is a spy for Prince Hydron and, along with Volt, an excellent tag team brawler. His guardian Bakugan is a Ventus Altair, and his Trap is a Wired. Wired and Altair can combine into the deadly Meta Altair.

KOMBA

Komba was Julie's neighbor in Africa. His guardian Bakugan is a Ventus Harpus, which he lost in season 1 thanks to Masquerade. He wants to train under Shun so that he can become a better brawler.

SUBTERRA

Subterra's a rugged planet, both above and below ground.
Like the hard planet they come from, Subterra Bakugan are rock solid
and tough to the core! They never turn away from a fight, and,
once in a fight, they give their all to crush opponents.
Talk about a force as strong as stone!

Subterra is all about big G-Power: straightforward, stomping attacks that leave your opponent wondering why their clever tricks weren't enough to win the game. Success comes to the Subterra player by taking a no-holds-barred approach to monster G-power.

THE SUBTERRA BAKUGAN

Unlike most Attributes, a lot of Subterra's power comes directly from the Bakugan, which feature higher G-Powers than the other Attributes. So for Subterra, go with the three biggest G-Powers that you have. This means you may lose one battle from an opponent's clever trick, but hopefully, you'll win the rest!

THE GATE CARDS

Silver

Using cards that give a great bonus for Subterra while not giving much to other Attributes is certainly one way to go, but there are other good choices. Sometimes an opponent will use a Trap to get a better Gate bonus. To defend against tricks like that, try a card like High Energy or Cavern Portal. I also really like the card Flybeetle Rescue.

Gold

For your gold Gate card, you can go a couple of different ways. There are two great choices if you're using a Gorem: Gorem and Under Current. And check out any and all Gate cards that stop Ability cards from being played, like Crushing Blow.

Copper

Stay away from those "lowest G-Power wins" cards—you want to keep the battle as straightforward as possible. Shades of Death and Pounce would both work if you know your opponent is only using one Attribute. Field of Dread is good, too, if you think you can get the battle to happen when you don't have any Traps in your used pile.

Red

Rikimaro's Surprise is one of my personal favorite red Ability cards for Subterra. It helps you completely avoid the bad effects of your opponent's tricky Gate cards. Call of the Hex is an excellent combo with Field of Dread, and Mira and Shun is a fantastic card that also allows a re-roll.

"Subterra is probably the best Attribute for beginning players, but still an excellent choice for even the most experienced Bakguan master!"

Bakugan Tournament Master Josh

Blue

For your blue Ability card, go for a generically useful G-Power boost, like Soil Mana. It's a solid bonus that works on all Gate cards, and sometimes gives an extra 120 G-Power. But there are a lot of good choices here; try and experiment to find what you like.

Green

For green, Subterra is a classic way to, if not win, then at least avoid losing! Shadow Lash can stop your opponent from gaining those super high Gate bonuses from his own Gate cards. And since you are likely to win a battle or two by a large margin, Subterra Vexos is a great choice, too.

Subterra doesn't require nearly as much finesse as the other Attributes, so it's a little more forgiving if you make a mistake in the game. When I play Subterra I rarely win all of the first three battles, it is almost always a pretty close game. I can't stop all of my opponent's crazy tricks, but if I can stop one or two, it's usually enough to win. The only Attributes I tend to have problems beating are Ventus, as they move everything all over the place, and Haos with its big come-from-behind effects. If you're just starting out or are introducing a friend to Bakugan, they might want to play Subterra as it is the most straightforward Attribute.

SUBTERRA CRUSHERS

There are quite a few cards you should consider for a Subterra force if you think you are going to have a lot more G-Power at some battles than your opponent. If you've got some really high G-Power Subterra Bakugan, it gives you the flexibility to try some of these cards!

SUB TERRA 2

Play at the start of a battle where you have a Sub Terra Bakugan™, if you win the battle by at least 150 G-Power, put one of your unused Gate cards into the arena in place of the Gate card you just won.

Joue au début d'une bataille lorsque tu as un Bakugan™ Sub Terra. Si tu gagnes la bataille par au moins 150 points de Puissance G, place une de tes cartes Portail non utilisées dans l'arène à la place de la carte Portail que tu viens de gagner.

BA242-AB-SM Bakugan™ 2008 Spin Master LTD. & SEGA Toys 47/48b

GROUND

Play at the start of a battle where you have a Sub Terra Bakugan™. Reduce all the Attribute bonuses printed on the Gate card that are higher than 50 to 50.

Joue au début d'une bataille où tu as un Bakugan™ Sub Terra. Tous les bonus d'Attribut de la carte Portail qui sont supérieures à 50 sont réduits à 50.

BA289-AB-SM Bakugan™ Spin Master Ltd. © Sega Toys/Spin Master 46/48c

SUB TERRA

Play after you lose a battle with a Sub Terra Bakugan™ by less than 100 G-Power. The winning player doesn't win the Gate card. Instead, the Gate card remains in the arena and the Bakugan™ go to their owner's used piles.

Joue après avoir perdu de moins de 100 points de Puissance G une bataille avec un Bakugan™ Sub Terra. Le gagnant ne gagne pas la carte Portail; elle demeure dans l'arène et le Bakugan™ va dans la pile "Hors Jeu" de son propriétaire.

BA179-AB-SM Bakugan™ 2008 Spin Master LTD. & SEGA Toys 47/48

STUCK

Play before you roll a Sub Terra Bakugan™. If this roll results in a battle, any G-power bonuses from Ability cards are reduced to zero.

Joue avant de lancer un Bakugan™ Sub Terra. Si le lance provoque une bataille, tout bonus de Puissance G de cartes Capacité est réduit à zéro.

BA227-AB-SM Bakugan™ 2008 Spin Master LTD. & SEGA Toys 32/48b

FIRE STONE™

Play before you roll a Sub Terra or Pyrus Bakugan™. Roll twice; if you stand on the same Gate card both times, no Gate bonuses or Ability card bonuses apply in battles this turn. Otherwise, you miss.

Joue avant d'avoir lancé un Bakugan™ Sub Terra ou Pyrus. Lance deux fois. Si tu te trouves sur la même carte d'entrée deux fois de suite, il n'y aura pas de bonus d'entrée ou de bonus de carte de capacité pour les combats de cette partie. Sinon, tu rates.

BA556-AB-SM-GBL-29 Bakugan™ Spin Master Ltd. ©2008 Sega Toys/Spin Master 20/48n

MIRA

Mira isn't just strong in battle, she's a strong leader, too. As the head of the Bakugan Brawlers Resistance, she had to get creative to fight the Vexos. Her guardian Bakugan is a Subterra Thunder Wilda, and her main Trap is a Baliton.

GUS

Gus is constantly training, and very loyal to Spectra, so much so that he is often called "Spectra's little pet" by the other members of Vexos. His guardian Bakugan is a Subterra Vulcan, and his main Trap is a Hexados.

BILLY

Billy is Julie's friend from childhood and battled in season 1 under the control of Masquerade. Once, he almost sent both Julie and Gorem to the Doom Dimension!

HAOS

The radiant planet of Haos is unique. The center of the planet is a massive source of power, which draws energy from all sources of light. It is on this planet that the Haos Bakugan have discovered the mythical ability to control and manipulate light and energy. Never count Haos out of a fight: when things look dismal, they can "brighten" the odds, leaving opponents dazed and defeated.

Unlike the brute force of Subterra or the tricky movement of Aquos, Haos uses the power of light to win in surprise come-from-behind battles.

THE HAOS BAKUGAN

You'll want to take special care when picking your Bakugan, as so many of your special abilities involve snatching victory from the jaws of defeat. If you play the biggest Bakugan you have, you might not be able to use your special powers!

THE GATE CARDS

Silver

When I play Haos, I tend to go for the biggest Haos bonus I can get without too much thought as to what the other Attributes gain. I'll take the risk that the Gate card might give my opponent a decent bonus, as long as I can guarantee that it gives me a big bonus. I like to play with Sun Spot, Light-Burst, or Baked Soil.

Gold

For your gold Gate card, you will likely want to include one that matches one or more of your Bakugan. Many of those cards, like Wavern, give you your Gate bonus again. Another great choice is Recharge, which gives you a great bonus and can help you reuse an Ability card. Just make sure you have played enough Ability cards before the battle starts to get the special ability!

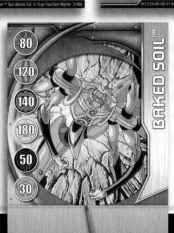

Copper

Copper Gate cards are custom-made to support the coming-from-behind theme of Haos. They are all about swapping G-Powers like the aptly-named G-Power Swap, having the lowest G-Power win like Short Fuse, or giving some other benefit to the lowest printed G-Power. Mirror Gate provides a way to reuse an Ability card, plus it has an excellent Haos bonus.

Red

Runo's Throw is a good choice if you are using a wide variety of G-Power Bakugan. Ace and Baron is one of the few red cards that gives a G-Power bonus. But my favorite card here is Mirror Play, as it's easy to fall behind early, and a card like this makes it easy to win on an opponent's Gate.

G-POWER SWAP

70 / 90 / 130 / 130 / 100 / 60

The Bakugan™ have their printed G-Powers swapped.

Les Bakugan™ échangent leur Puissance G.

BA260-GA-SM Bakugan™ © Sega Toys/Spin Master. 17/48c

SHORT FUSE

150 / 200 / 180 / 120 / 220 / 110

The Bakugan® with the lowest G-Power wins this battle.

Le Bakugan® qui a la Puissance G la plus basse gagne ce combat.

BA647-GA-SM-GBL Bakugan® Spin Master Ltd. ©2009 Sega Toys/Spin Master Ltd. 17/48g

RUNO'S THROW

Play before you roll. You may roll a Bakugan™ from your used pile this turn (you still only roll one Bakugan™ this turn).

Joue avant de lancer. Tu peux lancer un Bakugan™ de ta pile "Hors Jeu" lors de ce tour (attention, tu ne peux jouer qu'un seul Bakugan® pendant ce tour).

BA139-AB-SM Bakugan™ 2008 Spin Master LTD. & SEGA Toys 27/48

ACE and BARON

Play before you roll a Haos or Darkus Bakugan®. If it stands and is in a battle this turn, your Bakugan gets +50 G-Power. If you miss, you may re-roll it one time, but it will not get the G-Power bonus.

Joue avant de lancer un Bakugan® Haos ou Darkus. Si ton Bakugan est placé et si un combat a lieu pendant ce tour, ton Bakugan obtiendra +50 de Puissance G. Si tu rates le tir, tu peux relancer ton Bakugan une fois de plus mais il n'obtiendra pas de Puissance G.

BA600-AB-SM-GBL Bakugan® Spin Master Ltd. ©2009 Sega Toys/Spin Master Ltd. 24/48

MIRROR GATE

100 / 0 / 120 / 190 / 90 / 160

The player who has the Bakugan™ with the lowest printed G-Power may return any one Ability card he plays this turn to his unused pile after the battle.

Le joueur qui a le Bakugan™ avec la Puissance G qui peut déplacer n'importe quelle carte Capacité jouée ce tour dans sa pile "non-utilisée" après le combat.

BA460-GA-SM-GBL-21 Bakugan™ Spin Master Ltd. ©2008 Sega Toys/Spin Master Ltd. 27/48

MIRROR PLAY

Play before you roll a Haos Bakugan® if you don't have the most Gate cards in your used pile. Before battles this turn, Bakugan swap printed G-Power and attributes.

A jouer avant de lancer un Bakugan® Haos si tu n'as pas le plus grand nombre de cartes Portail dans ta pile Hors Jeu. Avant le combat pendant ce tour, ton Bakugan échange sa Puissance G imprimée contre ses attributs.

BA657-AB-SM-GBL Bakugan® Spin Master Ltd. ©2009 Sega Toys/Spin Master Ltd. 27/48

Blue

For your blue Ability card, look for a big Haos bonus like Flash. Remember that you will likely be starting below your opponent in G-Power, so go ahead and pick one of the harder-to-use ones. I think the best blue G-Power bonus cards for Haos are The Glow and Sneak — great bonuses and easy to use for most Haos players.

Green

Haos 2 has got to be one of the top five most powerful cards in the game. Very few other cards let you move Gate cards from your enemy's used pile to yours. There are other great choices too though. See the Light is one of few green G-Power bonus cards. Cards like Blinding Reflection are good on enemy Gate cards. Never Give Up! is good as well, because when you lose a battle, you'll tend to lose it big.

More than most Attributes, it is critical that you play through your strategies a few times to get a better feel for when certain cards should be deployed. With a Haos force, it's often okay to let your opponent win a battle, giving you an edge later in the game. Be extra careful with a Haos force when going up against Subterra, as many of the Subterra abilities can shut down your clever tricks.

"A true master knows the strengths and weaknesses of each Attribute."

Bakugan Tournament Master Luke

CARD FOCUS: RELISH VICTORY

Haos requires timing. Sometimes, you'll intentionally lose early battles that you might have been able to win to give you the advantage later.

Relish Victory is a card that can easily turn an important battle late in the game, but if you play all your Ability cards early, it won't work. If you include Relish Victory in your force, it'll change the way you play, what other cards you use, and what balls you play.

When I play this card, I make sure to avoid copper Gate cards that let the lowest G-Power win, and instead pick one that swaps G-Power. This will likely make my opponent play some Ability cards to raise his own G-Power to win the battle, and I'll let him! Then later, I'll play Relish Victory for a huge bonus and I'll have saved my other cards to play late in the game.

Relish Victory is just one Haos card that will affect how you play. Try others and your strategy will evolve along with your playing style.

RELISH VICTORY

Play during a battle. Increase the Haos Gate Attribute bonus by 150 G-Power for each Ability card in your opponent's used pile that's less than the number in yours at the end of the battle.

À jouer pendant un combat. Augmente le Bonus d'Attributs de Portail Haos de +100 de Puissance G pour chaque carte Maîtrise que ton adversaire possede en moins que toi dans sa pile Hors Jeu à la fin du combat.

BA764-AB-SM-GBL Bakugan® Spin Master Ltd. ©2009 Sega Toys/Spin Master Ltd. 45/48ah

POPULAR HAOS BRAWLERS

VOLT
Volt is part of the Vexos organization, and a tough brawler to beat. He even defeated Dan early on in New Vestroia. His Guardian Bakugan is a Haos Brontes and he uses a Dynamo Trap.

RUNO
At the end of the first season, Runo and Dan start to date. Her Guardian Bakugan is a Tigrerra that evolved into a Blade Tigrerra. She appears in New Vestroia as well as the first season. When not battling, she helps her parents run a restaurant.

BARON
He is the youngest member of the Bakugan Brawlers Resistance in New Vestroia. He is a big fan of the original brawlers. Originally, he fought with a Tigrerra, but lost her in a battle. Now his guardian Bakugan is a Haos Mega Nemus, and his preferred Trap is a Piercian.

Sometimes it's fun to play a force that uses Bakugan of more than one Attribute. This will almost always surprise your opponent, and it makes it very hard for your opponent to guess which tricks you have up your sleeve.

There are quite a few cards that support this type of force, and if you try these out, you'll realize that certain Attributes tend to work well together. Here's a look at some of the pieces that work particularly well when you play Bakugan of more than one Attribute. There are a LOT more cards than these, but the cards here should be enough to get you started.

Variety's Curse is a Gate card that only allows mixed Attribute players to play Ability cards. It is good for a Subterra and Ventus force.

Cards like Triangle of Power give bonuses for multiple Attributes, so they can be great blue card choices for you.

Rainbow and the three "Tri-Color" cards are more great Gate cards, all with a built-in bonus for mixed Attribute players.

And if you're using one or more Ingrams, you should look at the Green Ability card Ingram Beam.

There are some card sub sets that were released that you should definitely look at when you make mixed Attribute forces. For instance, if you are using Ventus as one of your Attributes, you can pick from "X" Wind cycle. If you want to put a little Darkus in your force, you could pick from the Shadow series, which is really good in the big game or a multiplayer game.

These cards can be used in single Attribute forces effectively, too, but it's nice to be able to put them into mixed Attribute forces, as there is no downside.

FIRE WIND™

Play after you roll and stand a Ventus or Pyrus Bakugan™. You may move any standing Bakugan to any Gate card.

Joue après avoir lancé et placé un Bakugan™ Ventus ou Pyrus. Tu peux déplacer n'importe quel Bakugan vers n'importe quelle carte d'entrée.

WATER WIND™

Play after you roll and stand a Ventus or Aquos Bakugan™. You may move any standing Bakugan to any Gate card.

Joue après avoir lancé et placé un Bakugan™ Ventus ou Aquos. Tu peux déplacer n'importe quel Bakugan vers n'importe quelle carte d'entrée.

LIGHT WIND™

Play after you roll and stand a Ventus or Haos Bakugan™. You may move any standing Bakugan to any Gate card.

Joue après avoir lancé et placé un Bakugan™ Ventus ou Haos. Tu peux déplacer n'importe quel Bakugan vers n'importe quelle carte d'entrée.

DARK WIND™

Play after you roll and stand a Ventus or Darkus Bakugan™. You may move any standing Bakugan to any Gate card.

Joue après avoir lancé et placé un Bakugan™ Ventus ou Darkus. Tu peux déplacer n'importe quel Bakugan vers n'importe quelle carte d'entrée.

SHADOWFIRE™

Play during a battle if you have a Darkus or Pyrus Bakugan™ on an opponent's Gate. Your opponent's Bakugan gets no Attribute bonuses from the Gate.

A jouer pendant un combat si tu as un Bakugan™ Darkus ou Pyrus sur un Portail d'un adversaire. Le Bakugan de ton adversaire n'obtient aucun bonus d'Attribut de Portail.

SHADOW VORTEX™

Play during a battle if you have a Darkus or Ventus Bakugan™ on an opponent's Gate. Your opponent's Bakugan gets no Attribute bonuses from the Gate.

A jouer pendant un combat si tu as un Bakugan™ Darkus ou Ventus sur un Portail d'un adversaire. Le Bakugan de ton adversaire n'obtient aucun bonus d'Attribut de Portail.

SHADOW LASH™

Play during a battle if you have a Darkus or Sub Terra Bakugan™ on an opponent's Gate. Your opponent's Bakugan gets no Attribute bonuses from the Gate.

A jouer pendant un combat si tu as un Bakugan™ Darkus ou Sub Terra sur un Portail d'un adversaire. Le Bakugan de ton adversaire n'obtient aucun bonus d'Attribut de Portail.

RAIN OF SHADOWS™

Play during a battle if you have a Darkus or Aquos Bakugan™ on an opponent's Gate. Your opponent's Bakugan gets no Attribute bonuses from the Gate.

A jouer pendant un combat si tu as un Bakugan™ Darkus ou Aquos sur un Portail d'un adversaire. Le Bakugan de ton adversaire n'obtient aucun bonus d'Attribut de Portail.

BONUS GOODIES!

This section is filled with bonus features. There's instructions on how to run a fun Bakugan tournament, and even a fun look at some season 3 material!

Ready to test out your skills? Then it's time for a Bakugan brawler tournament! There are all sorts of formats for tournaments; here is a fairly easy one to run. We've even included a prize certificate in this book that you can copy and fill out for the winner. Armed with these rules, you'll finally be able to find out who the best brawler in your area is—will it be you?

Players

You need at least four players for your tournament. The more players you have, the more time the tournament will take.

Rules

Before the tournament, all players should agree on which format will be used—normal game, big game, or multiplayer. I prefer four-player games, but if you don't have enough players for that, you can run them as one-on-one games. Each player should know the rules of Bakugan before playing in a tournament.

The Tournament Organizer

It's a good idea to have one player be in charge of the tournament. For small tournaments, it's okay for the tournament organizer to also play in the tournament. If you're running a big tournament (say, eight players or more) then it might be best if the tournament organizer doesn't play, but that's up to you.

The tournament organizer's job is to answer rules questions that may come up. If a question comes up, the tournament organizer has the final say, so the organizer should know the game really well.

The Tournament Cards

Each player needs an index card (or something similar). The tournament card is how each player keeps track of which opponents they have played, as well as how many points they've won. Each player should write their name at the top of their card.

Battle!

Time to battle! Each player should challenge a player that they haven't played yet. Before the game starts, each player writes down the name of their opponent on their tournament card.

After the game is over, each player records how many points they scored. Then the players challenge another player they haven't played yet (write their names down, score points, etc...). Once each player has played three games (or played all the other players), the tournament ends and the player with the most points wins!

Scoring

After each game, you get one point for each Gate card in your used pile at the end of the game. That means the winner of the game will get three points, while the loser will either get two, one, or no points. Be sure to write down your points right after the game — you might forget them if you write them down later.

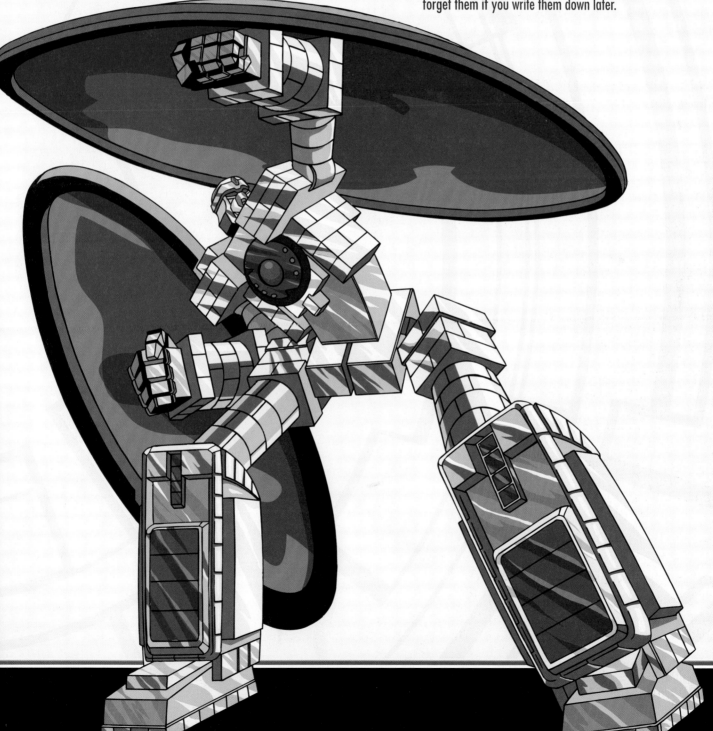

Winning the Tournament

The player who scored the most points gets first place, the next-highest score gets second, and so on.

What If?

What if more than one player is tied for first place at the end of the tournament?

The tournament organizer can declare a tie, or have them battle one more time.

What if we run out of time before each player has finished playing all the other players?

Just put your tournament cards in a safe place, and continue the tournament when you have more time.

For the Tournament Organizer

If you get a rules question, do your best to make a fair ruling. It often helps to read the card text out loud, as most rules questions can be answered by reading the whole card. If you are totally stumped, flip a coin to decide — it's important to keep the tournament moving! Then note down the question and ask the question on the forums at bakugan.com to get an official answer. If a rules question comes up in a game you are playing in, have a player not in the game make the ruling.

The hardest part of your job happens when someone is accused of cheating. If this happens, listen to both sides of the story, and again, try to be fair. Most of the time, the person wasn't cheating, they were just making mistakes and playing wrong. In the rare case that someone was actually cheating on purpose, they should be dropped from the tournament. Above all, be fair, and keep the tournament moving. It's not fun to stop the tournament to resolve a problem, so make your decision and let the game continue.

TOURNAMENT CHAMPION!

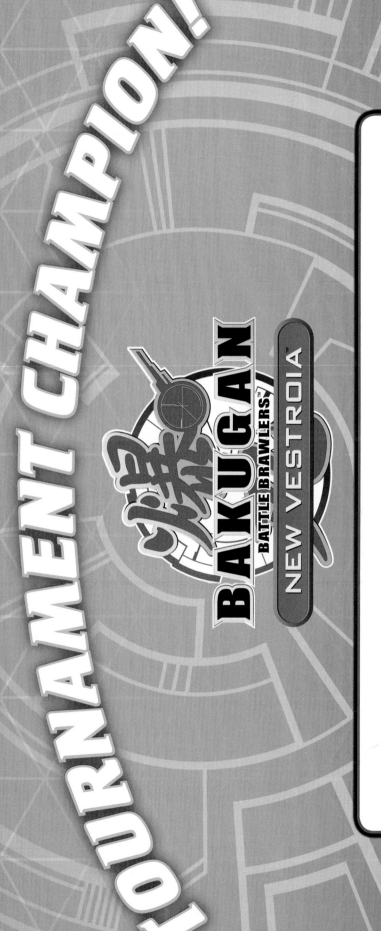

THIS AWARD CERTIFIES THAT

_____
(NAME)

HAS WON THE BAKUGAN TOURNAMENT AT

_____
(LOCATION)

ON

_____
(DATE)

CONGRATULATIONS, YOU'RE ON YOUR WAY
TO BECOMING A TRUE BAKUGAN MASTER.

BAKUGAN
BATTLE BRAWLERS
NEW VESTROIA

Every few months, a new set of Bakugan are available in stores, but there are a few super-exclusive Bakugan that have come out. I'm always asked what are the rarest Bakugan. Here are some of those very hard-to-find Bakugan:

Gold Fear Ripper

This is a Haos Fear Ripper that was made in a golden color. This was a promotional Bakugan given away at a very small number of promotional events in Canada. This product was made before the rules were updated, so their cards don't work in the game, but honestly, if you get one of these, I'd think twice before taking it out of the package.

Comic-Con 2009 Promotion

Spin Master produced a BakuSteel Neo Dragonoid that was only available at the 2009 San Diego Comic-Con. The package came with a really cool figurine as well. Twelve hundred of these were numbered and released to the public. Other than a few production samples, those are all that exist! A super rare Bakugan for sure!

Super Special Attacks

There were two special attack Bakugan released near the end of the New Vestroia Bakugan. These were available in stores, but only in very small quantities and only for a very limited time. These are the electronic Bakugan — Moonlit Monarus and Flare Wilda. If you were lucky enough to find these on a shelf, you were very lucky.

A LOOK AT SEASON 3

By the time you get this book, there will be a bunch of products from season 3 at your local store, and likely, in your collection. Season 3 features some amazing Bakugan and special attack Bakugan, but the two big new things in season 3 are Battle Gear and the hard to find "Evolution" Bakugan.

HELIX DRAGONOID

DHARAK

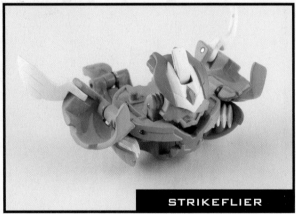

STRIKEFLIER

LUMAGROWL

PHOSPHOS

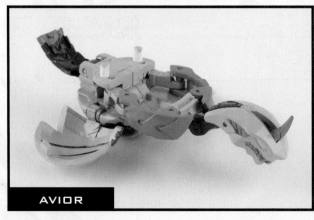

AVIOR

Battle Gear

Battle Gear are played during combat and give a G-Power bonus. Each one comes with a reference card that describes additional bonuses of the Battle Gear based on your Bakugan's Attribute. Many Bakugan in season 3 are designed so that the Battle Gear opens right on top of the Bakugan!

BATTLE TURBINE

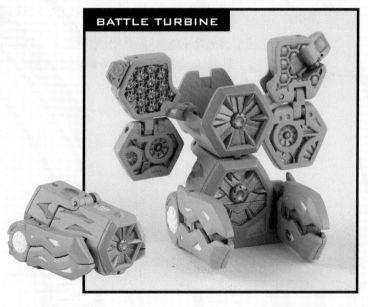

JETKOR

TERRORCREST

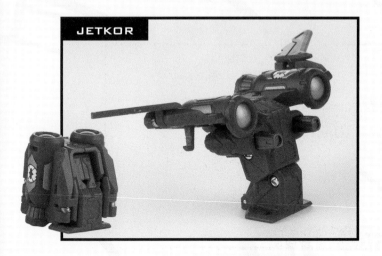

BARIAS GEAR

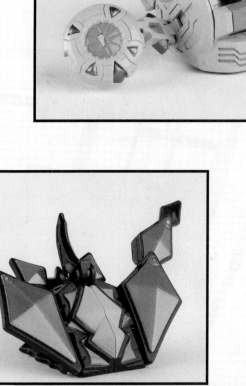

AIRKOR

Evolution Bakugan

Evolution Bakugan are in the special attack section of the store. They are super-high G-Power Bakugan, but they don't start the game in play. Instead, you have to wait until certain conditions are met, then you can swap one of your Bakugan with your Evolution Bakugan. All of that information is on a reference card that comes with the Evolution Bakugan, where you will also find a built-in special ability!

Look for ways to incorporate the new season 3 enhancements into your game strategy! It's all part of the journey to becoming a Bakugan master!